Haunted
Hoops
Shadow

Spellbound

An Imprint of Magic Wagon
abdopublishing.com

By Rich Wallace Illustrated By Dave Shephard

abdopublishing.com

Published by Magic Wagon, a division of ABDO, PO Box 398166,
Minneapolis, Minnesota 55439. Copyright © 2017 by Abdo
Consulting Group, Inc. International copyrights reserved in all
countries. No part of this book may be reproduced in any form
without written permission from the publisher. Spellbound™ is a
trademark and logo of Magic Wagon.

Printed in the United States of America, North Mankato, Minnesota.
052016
092016

Written by Rich Wallace
Illustrated by Dave Shephard
Edited by Heidi M.D. Elston
Designed by Laura Mitchell

Publisher's Cataloging-in-Publication Data

Names: Wallace, Rich, author. | Shephard, David, illustrator.
Title: Hoops shadow / by Rich Wallace ; illustrated by David Shephard.
Description: Minneapolis, MN : Magic Wagon, [2017] | Series: Haunted
Summary: After the first day of tryouts for the school basketball team, Stu stays
    behind to shoot extra free throws, but when he's about to leave, he encounters
    a strange boy wearing an old basketball uniform.
Identifiers: LCCN 2016936524 | ISBN 9781624021480 (lib. bdg.) |
    ISBN 9781680779639 (ebook)
Subjects: LCSH: Ghost stories. | Haunted houses--Fiction. | Basketball--Fiction.
Classification: DDC 813.6--dc23
LC record available at http://lccn.loc.gov/2016936524

Table of Contents

Chapter 1

Missed Shots

I wiped my *sweaty* forehead with the front of my T-shirt and tried to catch my BREATH. We'd been running forever. Coach was testing our GUTS.

I'd done well on this first day of basketball **tryouts**. I hoped I would make the team, but there were a lot of good **players**.

I **bounced** the ball. *Concentrate,* I thought. I was a good shooter, but I was **puffing** from all that running. My first shot *ROLLED* off the back of the rim. The second one fell short. My third shot **HIT** the front of the rim and dropped to the floor.

...ON, *Stu*, I thought.

...ne *shots*.

...fourth attempt *slipped*

...y *sweaty* fingers and missed

...a mile. I ended up making only

...vo out of ten.

TERRIBLE!

I shook my head. If I didn't improve tomorrow, I'd never make the team. Coach always STRESSED the importance of free throws.

"Free throws!" Coach called.

"Everybody shoot ten."

I waited in the LOCKER room until everyone left. Coach was in his office, so I SNUCK up to the gym. I needed extra practice.

I picked up a ball and headed for the line. **Bounced** it twice and shot.

Swish!

That was more like it.

I made four in a row. Then seven.

"Nice shooting," came a voice.

I JUMPED. I thought I was alone.

I turned and saw a kid my age. He was wearing a RETRO jersey with the number 25. I didn't recognize him. Maybe he was new.

"Your SHOOTING was off balance before," he said, walking toward me. "No matter how tired you are, you always have to be consistent."

The kid made a shot. "Take a **DEEP** breath before every free throw," he said. "Set your feet the same every time. Get it?" I **nodded**.

The kid looked around the **GYM**. "Come back later," he said. "I'll give you more tips."

"Tonight?" I said. "The gym will be LOCKED."

"I'll be here," he said. "I'll let you in."

Chapter 2
Randy

I walked the **quiet** streets back to the school that night. The place was **DARK** and empty. I shook my head and turned back for home.

"Get in here!" called the kid, *creaking* open the gym door.

I shrugged and walked in.

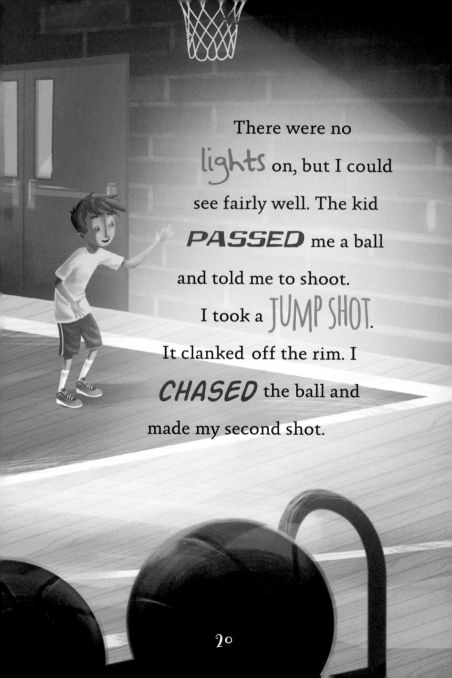

There were no *lights* on, but I could see fairly well. The kid **PASSED** me a ball and told me to shoot. I took a JUMP SHOT. It clanked off the rim. I **CHASED** the ball and made my second shot.

"Not bad," the kid said. "It's Stu, right?"

"Yeah."

"Call me Randy," he said.

We **SHOT** baskets for an hour.

"Is Mrs. Ward still teaching math here?" Randy asked.

"Never heard of her," I replied.

"How about Principal Johnson? Is he still a **GROUCH?**"

"I don't know Johnson either," I said. "When were they here?"

"When I was a student," he said. Randy didn't look any **older** than me. "How many years back?" I asked.

Randy didn't answer me.

I **RAN** in to grab a rebound.

"How long ago?" I asked again. But suddenly I realized I was ALONE.

"Randy?" I called. "You still here?"

My voice **ECHOED** in the empty gym.

**IN MEMORIAM
RANDY BLAKE**
1945 - 1957

Leading Scorer
1956 - 1957

Weird, I thought. I carried the ball
to the rack in the corner. Above the
rack was a **PLAQUE** on the wall.
I'd *never* looked closely
at it before.

Randy **DIED** more than half a century ago. I'd been **SHOOTING** baskets with a *ghost!*

Chapter 3
A Little Help

The next morning, I checked some old yearbooks. I found out Mrs. Ward retired more than fifty years ago. Mr. Johnson was principal until 1960.

Those dates fit with Randy Blake's time at the school. The 1957 yearbook was dedicated to him.

Had he been **HAUNTING** our gym

for all these years?

I looked for Randy during the second tryout session. There was no sign of him.

I did well in **dribbling** drills and a scrimmage. Made two steals and a couple of LAY-UPS.

The competition for spots on the team was TIGHT.

Coach blew his whistle.

"Free throws!" he said.

I gulped.

The other guards **SHOT** well.

When it was my turn, I let out my breath. **HARD**. My hands were shaking. *Be consistent*, I thought. That's what Randy had told me.

My first shot **bounced** high off
the back of the rim. It floated in space,
then FELL through the hoop! The
second one swished. Third one, too.

I **RAN** the streak to nine in a row. My tenth **SHOT** looked way off. At the last second, it *curved* toward the rim.

Made it!

I shook my fist. A few kids **CLAPPED**.

Coach said, "Great effort, Stu."

A few minutes later, Coach told me I'd made the *team*!

When I left the gym, Randy
was **WAITING** outside.

"Where were you?" I asked.

"I made it!"

"I know," he said with a smile.

"I helped a little."

"How?" I asked.

Randy laughed. "An extra NUDGE,"
he said. "A couple of tip-ins."

Then he faded away.

He was gone.

Chapter 4

25

That night I did some research.

An **old** newspaper headline said,

"BASKETBALL STAR KILLED IN CRASH."

He'd biked home from the final game.

DARK road.

SPEEDING car.

Long time ago. So sad.

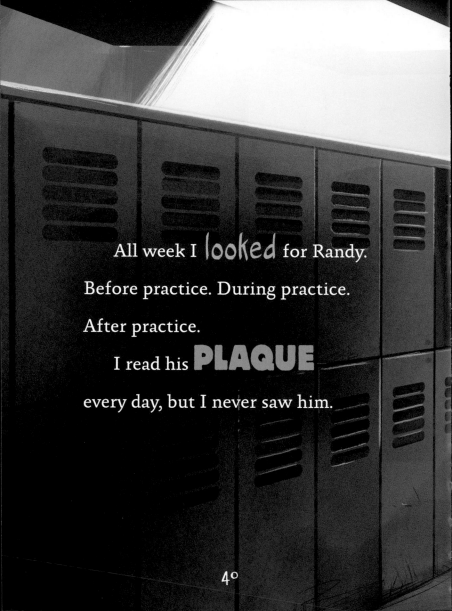

All week I looked for Randy.

Before practice. During practice.

After practice.

I read his PLAQUE

every day, but I never saw him.

Coach told me I'd play a lot in the games. I wouldn't be a starter, but I'd be one of the first players off the **BENCH**.

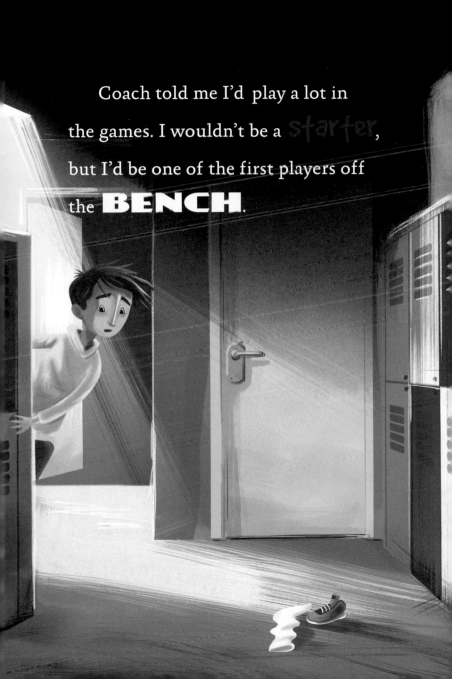

The night before our first game,
I stayed late to **SHOOT**. My mind
drifted off, and I couldn't hit a thing.

"Relax your wrist," came a
familiar voice.

"Where have you been, Randy?"

He SHRUGGED. "I come and I go." He took the ball and shot. "See? Relaxed wrist on the follow-through."

I tried it. Made five in a row!

I was feeling **CONFIDENT** when I got back to the locker room. Everyone was gone. I PEELED off my *sweaty* T-shirt and opened my locker.

"Stu," Coach said. He was HOLDING up three jerseys. The numbers were 12, 17, and 25.

"Pick one."

That was an *easy* choice.

We built a **BIG** lead in the opening game. I had five points when I took a **HARD** foul. The clock showed fifteen seconds left to play.

I 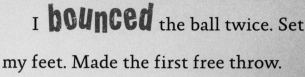 the ball twice. Set my feet. Made the first free throw. *"Perfect,"* came a CRY from the bleachers.

I gave Randy a thumbs-up. Then I SANK the second shot.